BERNARD WABER

I WAS ALL THUMBS

Houghton Mifflin Company
Boston

for JUSTIN

Printed in the United States of America

RNF ISBN 0-395-21404-1
PAP ISBN 0-395-53969-2

RNF HOR PAP B&B 10 9 8 7 6 5

Library of Congress Cataloging in Publication Data

Waber, Bernard.
  I was all thumbs.

  SUMMARY: An octopus who has known only the quiet
world of the laboratory tells of his unceremonious
introduction to the perils and pleasures of ocean life.

  [1. Octopus—Fiction] I. Title.
PZ7.W113Iae   [E]   75-11689

ISBN 0-395-21404-1

I was to be put into the sea.

Captain Pierre told me so.
He said:
"You will be happy there — in the sea.
It is where you belong."
I thought:
Thank you very much.
But what do I know of the sea?

I knew nothing of the sea.
My home, the only home I could remember,
was a tank in Captain Pierre's laboratory.

Now I will tell you a little something about this Captain Pierre.
Yes, he is the very same Captain Pierre who is so famous
for his undersea explorations.

He is also, alas, the same Captain Pierre I once considered
to be my dearest friend.
Listen to this: Captain Pierre wrote a book called *A Day
in the Life of an Octopus.* It was praised by everyone.
I, in turn, received no praise whatsoever for the many long
hours I spent helping him to write it; not even a thank-you note.
So much for friendship.

Now I will tell you something else about this Captain Pierre.
He is also famous for his jokes—once more, alas.
Listen to this: Captain Pierre called me Legs. And he
would say, for example: "How are you this morning, Legs?
Alive and kicking, I see—ha-ha-ha!
Well, keep on your toes today, Legs—ha-ha-ha!
Best foot forward—ha-ha-ha!"

Of course, I was not amused.
Nor would it have mattered to remind Captain Pierre
I have arms, arms, arms — not legs.
On the other hand (so to speak), I was not looking for adventure.
I was safe in my house of glass, and satisfied, too,
with long restful naps and excellent servings of shrimp,
lobster or crab when I awakened.
Why complain, I thought. Why make waves.
Leave well-enough alone.

But adventure looked for me.
It began swiftly, one morning,
when I was scooped up,
stuffed into a jar . . .

. . . and carried out to sea.
So this was it.
This was to be my thanks
for having taught Captain Pierre
all that he wished to know
about octopuses.
Goodbye! Good luck!
And out with the rubbish!

"You will be sorry for this foolishness, Captain Pierre!"
I cried out from within the jar.
"You have not yet learned all the ways of the octopus!
There are still mysteries, Captain Pierre . . . still questions
burning for answers!
There are secrets I take with me, Captain Pierre!
Oh, you will miss your friend the octopus, Captain Pierre!
I promise, you will cry a sea of tears for your loss!
In the name of science, Captain Pierre!
Captain Pierre! Captain Pierre! Capt. . . !"

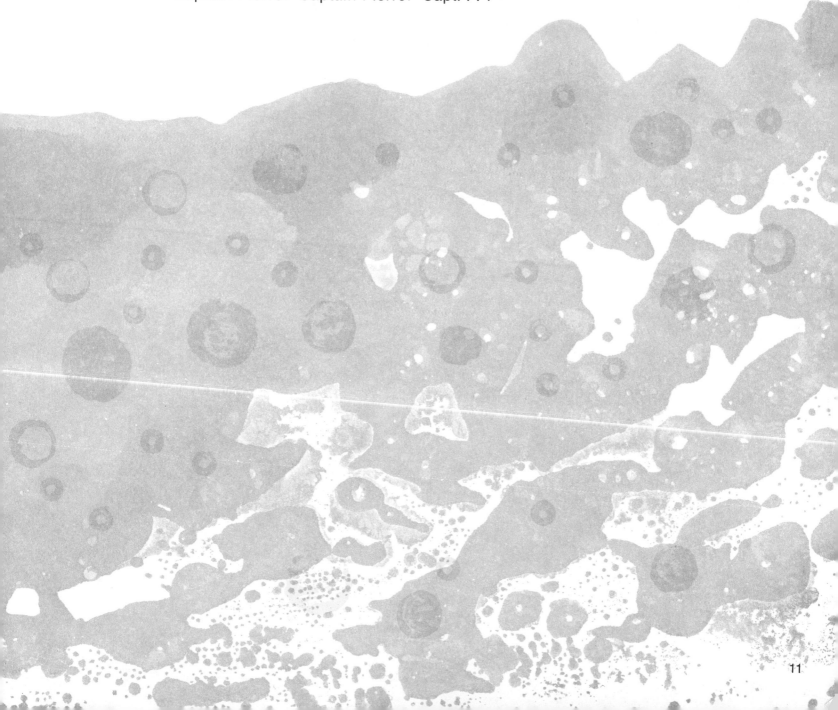

I wanted to have the last word, and I would have said more, had it not been for a thunderclap of a splash that sent me kicking, screaming and crashing, arm over arm, down to the strange new world of the sea.

I realized, at once, my arrival was not expected.
Everyone, it seemed, was staring.

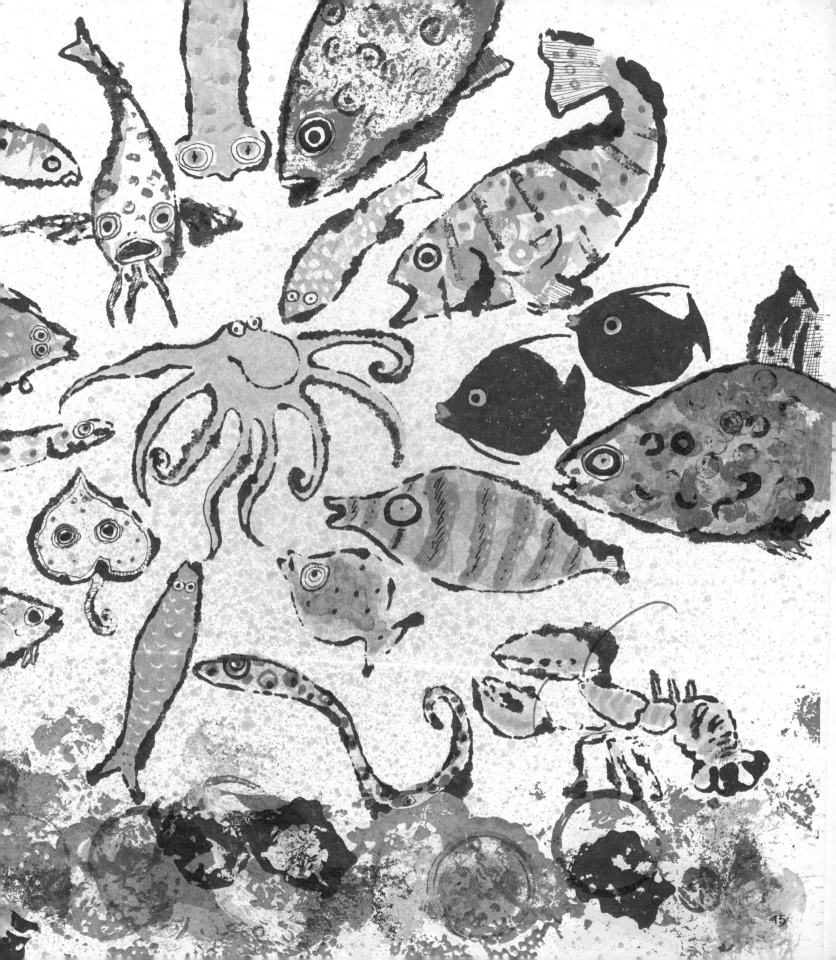

To make matters worse, I was in trouble from the start—
and all thumbs.

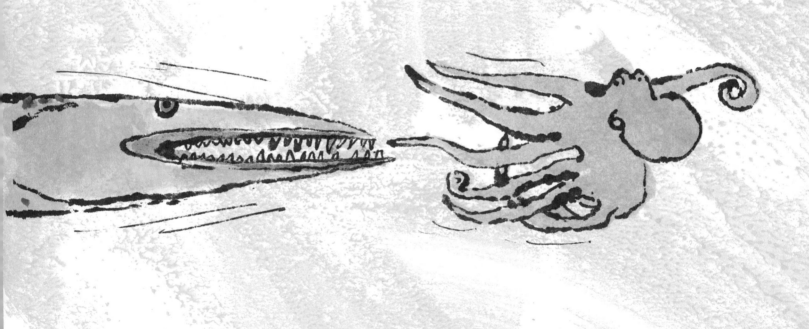

I turned red when I should have turned yellow.

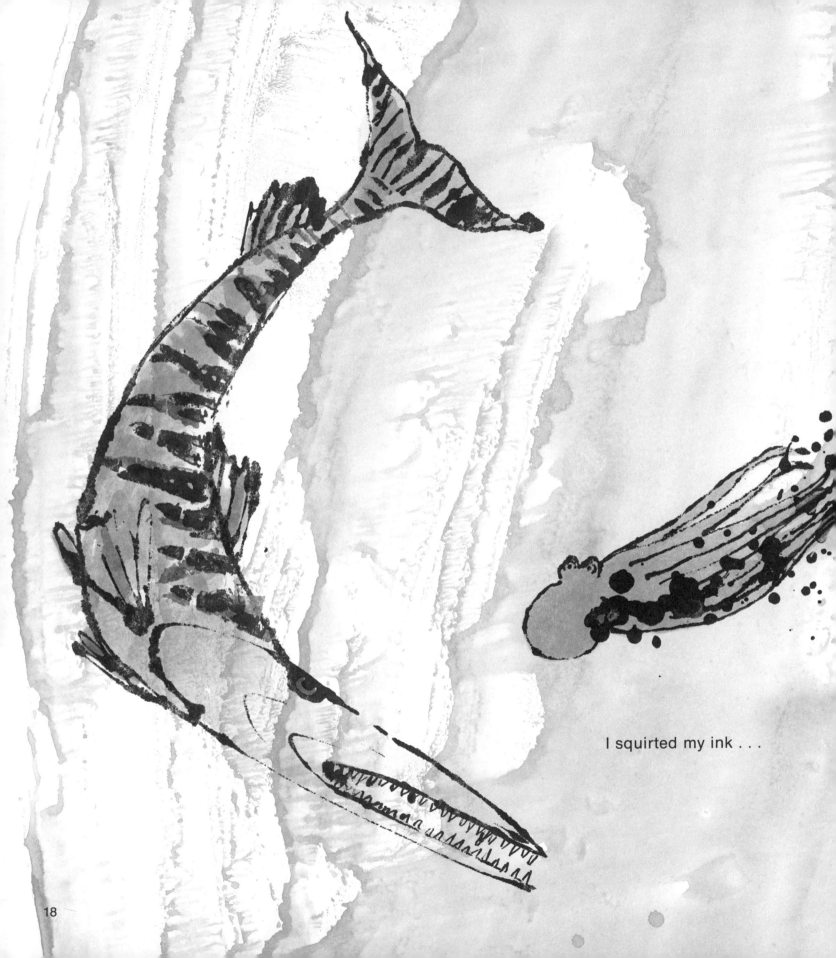

I squirted my ink . . .

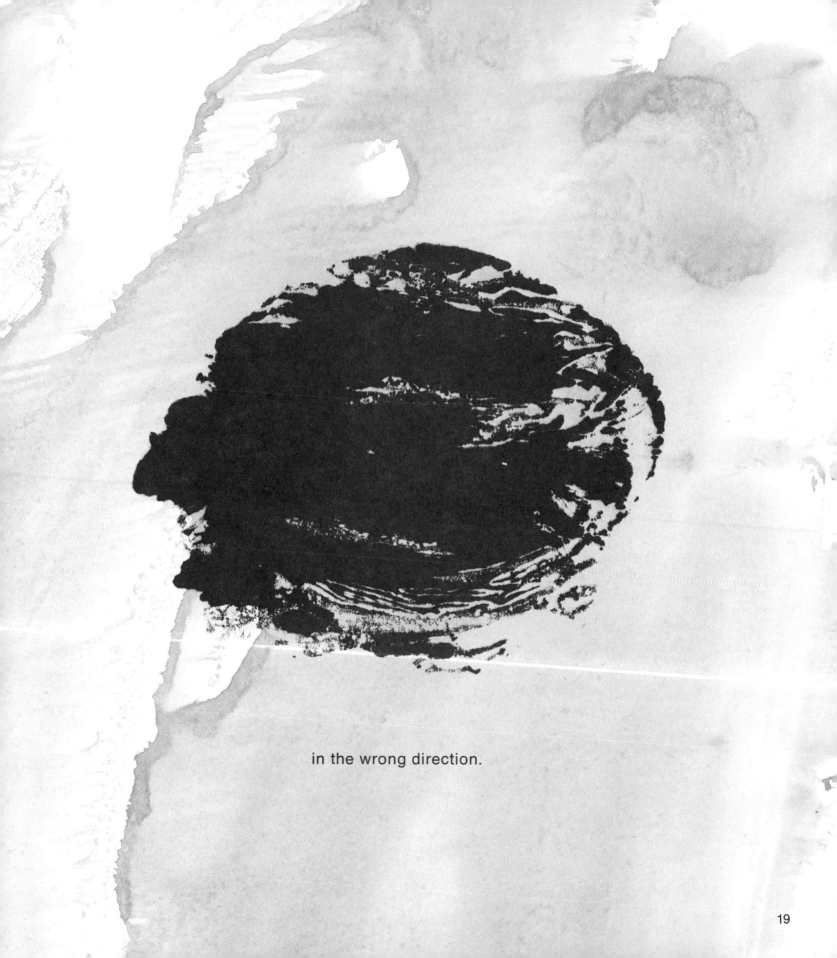

in the wrong direction.

I tripped all over myself and was so embarrassed I felt
just like crawling into a hole . . .
which I did . . .

the wrong hole.

I looked everywhere for a friendly face.

Luckily, I found a hiding place.
I needed time to think, time to pull myself together.
After a while, I began to wonder:
perhaps it was all my own fault.
Perhaps I was being foolishly shy.
Perhaps I should get out, be sociable, join a group.

So I joined a group.
And I told myself it was enormous fun and well worth the trip.
It was what follow-the-leader was really all about.

And I wiggled and I plopped.
And I zigged and I zagged.
And I rose and I dove—
just like everyone else.

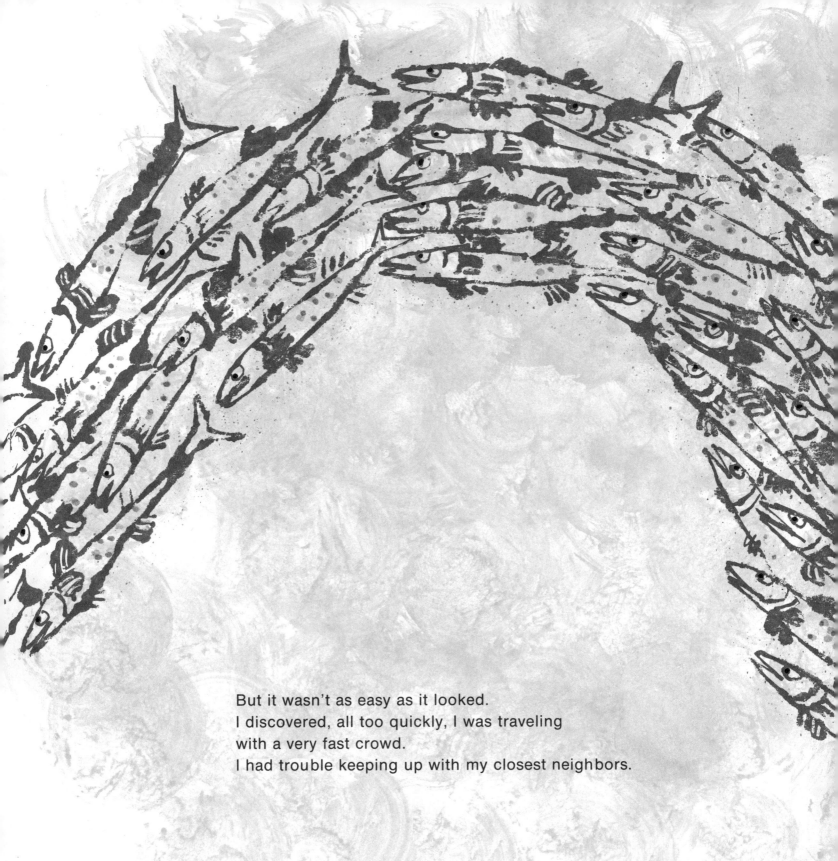

But it wasn't as easy as it looked.
I discovered, all too quickly, I was traveling
with a very fast crowd.
I had trouble keeping up with my closest neighbors.

In the end, it didn't matter.
One false turn and I was out—
footloose and alone again.

Now, more than ever, I wished for a friend.
I just wished some friendly someone would come to me and say:
"Hi, there! You're new around here aren't you?
I can tell by that lost expression on your face.
Well, let me be the first to welcome you to the sea.
Here, I'll show you around; introduce you to everybody.
Oh, you'll love the sea; really you will. We all do, you know.
Nice place—the sea.
I wouldn't dream of living anywhere else."

I was still thinking of this make-believe friend, when suddenly I heard a call for help. It came from a fisherman's trap close by. I looked into the trap, expecting to find a lobster, and had the surprise of my life. What I saw was not a lobster at all.
It was another octopus, but just as red as a cooked lobster.
"Please help me," cried the octopus.
"Why don't you squeeze through the opening," I suggested.
"I can't," the octopus answered, "I am stuffed to the gills with lobster."

"Here, I will help you," I said, grabbing a good hold
on the octopus.
"Push!" I called out as I pulled with all of my strength.
Suddenly, there was something like a popping sound
as the octopus, at last, burst free of the trap.

"What a relief!" the octopus cried out. "Are my eyes on straight?"
"Your eyes are fine," I answered.
"Well," said the octopus, "I am certainly thankful and
happy to meet you."
Immediately, I thought I had found a friend.
"I am happy to meet you, too," I said.

I began to tell the octopus all about myself.
"I lived with this Captain Pierre," I said. "We wrote
a book together."
"And he was always making jokes," the octopus interrupted.
"That's right!" I exclaimed. "But how did you know?"
"Because," said the octopus, "I, too, once lived with the
famous Captain Pierre."
"You did! You really did!" I exclaimed again.

"Well, isn't it a small world after all!"
"Yes, isn't it!" said the octopus.

"By the way," the octopus asked,
"what did Captain Pierre call you?"
"He called me Legs," I answered.
"I am not surprised," said the octopus.
"By the way," I asked,
"what did Captain Pierre call you?"
"He called me Knuckles," the octopus answered.
"I am not surprised," I said.

"Well!" said Knuckles, "one good turn deserves another.
Now that we are introduced, let me be the first to welcome
you to the sea. And I know the very spot where you will
want to settle down; a delightful place called Octopus-Metropolis.
There you will find empty tin cans, jars, bottles, tires,
shipwrecks, holes—all the many magnificent things that make
for true octopus happiness."
I was overcome.
"Please, dear friend, lead the way," I said.

We traveled for hours.
At last we reached Octopus-Metropolis.
It was everything Knuckles promised it would be; and more.

"But where are all the octopuses?" I asked. "I haven't seen one."
"You may not see them," Knuckles answered, "but they see you."
I looked again. There were row upon row of octopus houses.
Here and there an octopus arm stretched out and waved hello.
"Does each octopus live alone?" I asked.
"Yes," said Knuckles.
"Why is that?"
"Ah," Knuckles answered, "you still have a lot to learn
about octopuses."

"Look," said Knuckles, "how lucky for you! Here is an empty
house, a splendid size, too—with plenty of elbow room.
You can move in right now. My house is just down the way a bit."
"Say, Knuckles, why don't we live together and sort of keep
each other company?" I suggested.
"Sorry," said Knuckles, "it's just not the octopus way.
Each octopus must live alone. And Legs, let me give you a word of advice.
If ever you should think you might want to look in on another octopus
and say for example: 'Rise and shine!' or 'Come out,
come out, wherever you are!'"
"Yes?" I said.
"Well, don't. That would be considered very poor manners among octopuses.
And now, I am going home. Goodbye," said Knuckles.
"Goodbye," I said.

Knuckles started to move on, but stopped.
"Legs?"
"Yes, Knuckles," I answered.
"Drop around sometime."
"Oh, thank you, Knuckles. I most certainly will."

And so I settled down in my new house.
I watched Knuckles and the other octopuses
carefully, and this is what I learned.
I learned how to get my own dinner.

And I learned how to defend myself.
Now, I use my ink to good advantage.
Look! Now you see me . . .

POOF!!!
Now you don't.

41

Psssssst!!!
Here I am, safe and sound,
back in my octopus house.

I have never stopped being curious about the sea.
Each day brings new surprises.

One day, I had the biggest surprise of all.
I thought: what a strange fish!
I looked closer.
So, it was Captain Pierre!
Captain Pierre smiled. He was not able to speak,
but I could just imagine him saying:
"Well, Legs, I'll have to hand it to you, ha-ha-ha!
you certainly found yourself a home."

Captain Pierre raised his arm.
For a moment, I feared he had come to take me
back to the laboratory.
I prepared to escape.
Instead, Captain Pierre waved goodbye and swam away.

I stopped to admire a giant kelp.
Captain Pierre's words came back to me.
"You will be happy there—in the sea.
It is where you belong.
And I thought . . .

nice place—the sea.
I wouldn't dream of living
anywhere else.